# One False Move

## Dreda Say Mitchell

HODDER

First published in Great Britain in 2017 by Hodder & Stoughton
An Hachette UK company

2

A CIP catalogue record for this title is available from
the British Library

Paperback 978 1 473 64063 4
eBook ISBN 978 1 473 64064 1

Typeset in ITC Stone Serif Std by Palimpsest Book Production Limited,
Falkirk, Stirlingshire
Printed and bound by Clays Ltd, St Ives plc

Hodder & Stoughton policy is to use papers that are natural,
renewable and recyclable products and made from wood grown in
sustainable forests. The logging and manufacturing processes are
expected to conform to the environmental regulations of the
country of origin.

Hodder & Stoughton Ltd
Carmelite House
50 Victoria Embankment
London EC4Y 0DZ

www.hodder.co.uk

To libraries everywhere for doing such a fantastic job. Without the amazing and legendary Whitechapel Library I would never have become a writer.

# 1

9 p.m.

The attack came out of nowhere. One minute,
twenty-four-year-old Hayley Evans was stepping out of the piss-stained lift on the eighth
floor. The next, she was grabbed and slammed
into the wall. The impact sent a shockwave of
pain through her body. Air whooshed out of
her chest. She froze. Couldn't move. She knew
she should, but panic had set in. She'd always
wondered why victims didn't scream and fight
at times like this. But there was no fight in her.
Fear crawled down her spine as she looked at
her attacker. He was a blur of moving arms, his
dark clothing turning him into a shadow. The
black hoodie he wore flopped over his forehead
and was zipped high, masking most of his face.
He panted high and loud.

Something flashed and twisted in the electric
light. A knife. He shoved it under her long
jumper. Oh God, he wasn't going to . . .?
Hayley's blood ran cold. Her eyes grew wide

1

with horror. No way was she going to let him do that to her. No way. She fought back, using every dirty trick she had learned living on the Devil's Estate. She sprang off the wall like a tigress, taking him by surprise. Smashed her palms into his chest. And pushed with all her strength. He stumbled back in a strange, jelly-like dance. Hayley cried out with the ear-splitting power of a mad woman, just like her ex-boyfriend Adam had taught her. Noises caused confusion in your enemy, that's what he'd said.

Adam was right. The noise stopped the bastard in his tracks like he'd just met his worst nightmare. Hayley dodged to the side to get to the door to the stairs. Her breath was heavy and hard as she got closer and closer and— She yelped. Red-hot needles of pain tore through her scalp as he jerked her back by the hair. Her cries of pain turned to moans when he swung her round, yanking her head viciously back and down until she couldn't control her footing and fell on to the concrete.

Move! Move! But she couldn't. The pain was too strong and her vision kept coming and going. He loomed over her, his blade poised for action. He hunched down beside her. Shoved the knife under her jumper.

*I'm going to die. I'll never see my gorgeous Lily again.*

He cut a wild slice through the top of her jeans, going for something round her waist. And that's when Hayley knew what was happening. He had taken her money belt, where she stored the money she collected on her rounds.

For a brief second they both stared at the belt in his hands. And then he was gone.

Hayley lay there, dazed. She felt like sobbing her heart out. How much had been in the money belt? A thousand? Maybe a little more. Now it was all gone. The problem was, the money didn't belong to her. This job was meant to be her second chance. The start of her journey to a normal life after coming out of prison nine months ago. There weren't many people willing to employ someone who had just finished doing a stretch.

She'd been over the moon at finally landing a job with a genuine loan company. It wasn't ideal, but beggars couldn't be choosers. The job was simple. Every week she knocked on the doors of people on the estate who had taken out a loan and they paid it back to her a little at a time. The people who borrowed were the type who couldn't get help from banks for one reason or another. That's why most people called it getting money on the never-never.

Hayley had been doing the job now for four months without any trouble. So why had it gone so wrong tonight? She was street smart, always alert and checking over her shoulder to make sure that no one was following her on her rounds. She hadn't noticed anything unusual tonight. But she would bet her life that the robber had been spying on her for a while, carefully watching the route she took.

How else could he have known to wait for her on the eighth floor? She should know – she'd used that method in her previous bad-girl life too. It was the kind of thing that went on in the place nicknamed the Devil's Estate. Its real name was the Essex Lane Estate, and Hayley lived on it as well. It was well known for crime despite the residents being good people.

*'What do you expect, giving a jailbird like that a job handling cash?'* Hayley could already hear the disgusted, all-knowing whispers of people who didn't think ex-cons deserved another chance at life. They would probably point the finger at her. They would think she'd set up the robbery to get a cut of the cash. The old Hayley might have done that, but not the new. As soon as she'd stepped

4

through the prison gate she had vowed to go straight.

The door to the stairs opened. A surge of cold air swept over her, and she sighed with relief. Finally someone would help her. She started to speak, but whoever it was just stepped over her like she was a bag of rubbish and rushed inside one of the flats. They didn't even give her a second look. That was the problem with living on the Devil; people were so scared they didn't want to get involved.

Feeling stressed and crushed, Hayley managed to get to her knees and crawl over to where her shoulder bag lay dumped on the ground. Her purse was still there. And her mobile hadn't been stolen either. She pulled it out to call the police. But then she paused. Her finger hovered over the button but didn't press it. The last thing she needed was the cops in her life again. She could hear their accusing voices:

'Hello, Hayley. You down here again? Only just out, aren't you?'

'You were carrying a grand? Where the hell did you get a grand from? On the take already?'

No, the police weren't an option. Next she thought about calling her probation officer. She decided against that, too. He'd only start snooping in her life even more, and she could do without that, thank you very much.

She stood up slowly. Her body ached from the bruises on her back. Her jeans sagged on the left side where they had been cut. She pressed the lift button and less than a minute later was inside. She started to feel safe only when the metal doors shut with a hum and a bang. She slumped against the back wall, breathing deeply to steady her nerves. The lift lurched slightly as it reached the ground floor. When the doors opened Hayley's heart kicked into a fast beat again as she took baby steps forwards. She peeped out. She checked right. Checked left. Then she shot out and ran into the courtyard.

The tall and the small blocks of flats on the estate, with their hazy black outlines and watery yellow lights, whizzed past her. The night wind hit her face with invisible, chilly blasts. The booming bassline from a party in one of the buildings matched her own heartbeat. She kept running and running and running. Finally she stopped outside a ground-floor flat in a low-rise block.

Hayley hunted for her keys in her bag, but was trembling too much to find them. She hammered on the door. A curtain twitched in the kitchen window and someone looked out. A voice called out, 'Who is it?'

'Nanna Lisa, it's me.'

'Hayley?'

Two bolts were loosened on the heavy door. It opened slightly but was still held fast by a chain. When Nanna Lisa saw Hayley really was on her own, the door opened properly and she fell into her grandmother's arms.

'I've been robbed.' Hayley allowed herself to cry at last. With tears streaming down her face, she added, 'I've really screwed up this time.'

# 2

10 p.m.

'Have you called the police, love?' Nanna Lisa asked as they sat together in the sitting room.

Hayley was clutching a very strong cup of tea. Her grandmother had tenderly cleaned her bruises half an hour ago. Then she'd helped Hayley into her nightie and dressing gown.

Hayley arched her eyebrow. 'You know they're the last people I'd be calling.'

Nanna Lisa shook her white-haired head and tutted. 'You're not living on the wrong side of the law any more. They're there to help you.'

Nanna Lisa had once been a tall woman but now, at the age of seventy-three, she walked with a slightly bent back. Hayley adored her. She didn't know what she would do without her. Her grandmother had given Hayley and her younger brother Jamie a home when their mother, Nanna Lisa's daughter, had died. Maggie Evans had been struck down and killed by a drunk driver a week before her fortieth birthday.

The tragedy still made Hayley's heart wrench and brought a tear to her eye every time she thought about it. Her mum had been a good woman who hadn't deserved to die so young. Nanna Lisa had opened her arms to her grand-kids. She had fought like a tiger against Social Services, who had wanted to place her grand-children in foster care.

'I might be getting on, with a grey hair or two, but those two little ones are my flesh and blood and it's up to me to see them right,' she'd declared.

And when fifteen-year-old Hayley and eight-year-old Jamie had come to live with her in a three-bedroomed flat on the Essex Lane Estate, that's what she'd tried to do, as best she could. It wasn't her fault that Hayley had chosen the wrong boyfriend and started hanging around with the wrong crowd. Or that she'd got into all manner of trouble until finally she'd been locked up for three years. Her grandmother could've turned her back on her, but she hadn't. Hayley would for ever be grateful for that.

'What were you doing in Bell Tower?' Nanna Lisa asked. 'I didn't know any of your friends lived there.' She fixed Hayley with a beady stare. Hayley knew what the stare meant – her grandmother wanted the truth.

And the truth was Hayley had told her beloved Nanna Lisa a little white lie. She'd told her grandmother she'd found work behind the bar of one of the local pubs. If Nanna Lisa had realised she was collecting money, she would have been furious. The estate could be a dangerous place and she would have feared for Hayley's safety. Plus, that bad crowd Hayley had once been part of came out at night like vampires, and Nanna Lisa would be afraid that they'd suck her back into their world.

'I've been collecting money on the never-never,' Hayley confessed. Her hands tightened around her teacup, its warmth seeping into her skin.

'You what?' Nanna Lisa asked sharply. She slammed her cup down on the glass table. 'Have you lost your mind?'

Hayley put her own cup on the table. Her hands waved in the air as she defended herself. 'Come on, Nan, you know how hard it's been for me to get a job. I don't want to be on benefits for the rest of my days.' She finished with a plea. 'Please be happy that I've found work.'

Nanna Lisa's mouth tightened with disapproval. 'I've lived on this estate since it was built back in the seventies. Back then you could leave your door open; let your kids play out. Not any more. Now you've got to keep looking over your shoulder, what with all the drugs on the estate.' Her grandmother was right. Some big-time dealers were flooding the estate with drugs. Hayley and most of the other people who lived there had no idea who they were.

Nanna Lisa's eyes changed from annoyed to troubled. 'You aren't working for one of those dodgy loan sharks?'

Hayley shook her head. 'I'd never do that. It's a proper company. It's run by a sister and brother team. Mary Lewis is so nice. I haven't met her brother yet. I'll probably have to pay the money back over time, but I'm sure that Mary will be fine about it.'

Before Nanna Lisa could say anything else, a little voice piped up from the doorway. 'Mummy! Mummy!' Hayley's three-year-old daughter Lily stood in her jim-jams, her brown eyes lit up with joy and laughter.

Hayley opened her arms and her daughter flew into her lap. In that moment Hayley forgot all her troubles. Her darling Lily was the apple of her eye. She still felt an intense, deep shame that her precious daughter had been born in prison.

She'd never forget the day the prison doctor had told her she was pregnant. It had happened two months into her three-year sentence for her part in a warehouse robbery. It had shaken her world.

Instead of feeling proud like most mothers-to-be, she was terrified. Prison life was tough and could sometimes be violent. Not the type of world she wanted to bring an innocent baby into. She'd convinced herself things would only get worse. She got depressed and down. Even knowing that the prison had a mother and baby unit hadn't made her feel any better. Her life hit rock bottom. That was until one very special day. Hayley had been in the library, reading a magazine, when she'd had a funny feeling in her belly. It was like a tickle and flutter all rolled into one. She'd thought that something bad was happening and jumped up, distressed, to tell one of the other prisoners near her about it.

The other woman had chuckled and placed her hand gently on Hayley's arm. She'd said, 'That's your baby kicking for the first time.'

Stunned and surprised, Hayley had sat back down, looked at her belly in wonder and placed her hand over it. That's when she'd properly realised that she was carrying a real-life human being. A child needing love and care. A child who would look to her to find out how to live a decent life. A child needing a mum who would teach it right from wrong. What kind of mum would she be if she carried on in the dead-end world of crime? For the first time since she'd got banged up, Hayley's face had spread into a huge, happy smile. Suddenly the world didn't seem so scary. She'd whispered to her unborn child: 'I love you, my little angel. Mummy's going to make sure you have the best life ever.'

Those simple and heartfelt words became a vow about her own life. A vow to go straight and leave the bad times behind. Nanna Lisa had come to the rescue again when Lily reached the age when babies in prisons were taken from their mothers. She'd agreed to bring her up until Hayley had served her sentence. Handing Lily over had nearly broken Hayley's heart, but knowing she was being looked after by her wonderful grandmother had helped.

'Why aren't you in bed, young lady?' Hayley stroked her daughter's soft hair.

'Heard your voice,' Lily whispered. 'Wanted to see you.'

Hayley was thrilled. She was convinced that talking gently to her unborn baby first thing in the morning and last thing at night in her cell had forged the strong bond between them.

'Five minutes,' Hayley whispered back, 'then it's beddy-bye-time for you.'

The front door opened and slammed shut.

'Jamie, is that you?' Nanna Lisa called out.

'Who do you think it is?' came the gruff reply, 'Father Christmas?'

'Watch your mouth,' Hayley threw back, annoyed.

How dare he speak to their nan in that tone? Sometimes she wanted to strangle her brother. Jamie had more cheek and vinegar in him than a seventeen-year-old boy should be allowed.

'Leave him alone, love,' Nanna Lisa advised, trying to keep the peace.

Jamie had been such a lovely boy once, full of sparkle and laughter. But when he turned fifteen he'd turned into a teenage nightmare. He'd been thrown out of two schools for fighting and swearing, and nothing Hayley or Nanna Lisa said would make him go to a new one. Since then he'd been hanging around with a rough crowd on the estate and getting into all sorts of bother. Hayley knew she'd been a bad example and felt guilty about that. But

14

because of that she didn't want her baby brother ending up locked away in a secure unit for boys.

Jamie swaggered into the sitting room. He had the same brown hair as Hayley, but everything else was a mirror image of the father who had upped and left them when Jamie was three. His leaving was the reason they had both been so close to their mum.

'I hope you haven't been knocking about with the lads in that gang again,' Nanna Lisa warned him.

'Or Adam,' Hayley added.

Adam was her ex-boyfriend and Lily's father. Back in the bad old days, Adam had been her partner in crime. Jamie had looked up to Adam, the first older male figure in his life. 'Adam this, Adam that', was all Jamie had seemed to say.

At first Hayley had been grateful to Adam for taking Jamie under his wing. It made her smile to see the two men in her life so close. That was until the day she had seen Adam give Jamie a package, when he was just fourteen. In that moment she knew Adam was drawing her baby brother into his lawless world, just like he'd done to her. Hayley had felt both horror and a crushing guilt. Jamie would never have met

Adam if it hadn't been for her. After she got out of prison Hayley realised that Adam did not intend to leave his life of crime, so she cut all ties with him and made Jamie promise to stay away from him too.

'I told you I'm not seeing him any more,' Jamie answered, in a voice so angry it startled Hayley. 'What do you want me to do? Write it in blood on the wall?' And with that he stalked out. Speechless, Hayley gazed after him. She hadn't seen Jamie this angry since they buried their mother nine years ago. A few seconds later his bedroom door slammed.

'Leave him. Let him cool off,' Nanna Lisa said softly. 'I'll put Lily to bed.'

While her grandmother took Lily to the room she shared with her mum, Hayley knocked on Jamie's door. When she got no response, she opened it. Jamie lay on his back on his bed, staring at the ceiling. He looked so innocent, just like the child he had once been, the one who'd called her Lee-Lee because he couldn't say her name properly.

Hayley sat down next to him. 'I'm sorry. I didn't mean to upset you.'

He didn't say anything for a while, but then quietly let out, 'It's OK.'

'I need your help.'

Jamie sat up. 'What's happened?'

'I got mugged tonight—'

Before she could finish, Jamie stormed off the bed, his face red with fury. 'No one robs my sister. I'm going to find them and when I do I'm going to beat the crap out of them.'

Though Hayley was proud her brother wanted to defend her honour, she wouldn't let him attack another person, whatever they'd done. 'I don't want any trouble. I just need to get the money back. Can you give your friends a bell to see if they know who did it?'

Jamie took out his mobile and spoke to his friends for the next fifteen minutes. At last he said, 'Sorry, Hayley, no one knows anything. But I bet there's someone who can help you.'

'Who?'

'Adam. He'll know who did it. And if he can't find out who attacked you, he might give you the money.'

Hayley shot to her feet. 'Never. I will never take his dirty money.'

Besides, she told herself, she might still be worried but the important thing was that Mary Lewis would understand. Mary was a good woman.

# 3

9 a.m.

The sun was bright in the sky the following morning, but there was a chill in the air. Hayley wrapped up warm before going out to see her boss, Mary Lewis. The loan company was called Quids In and was just off the high street near the market. It was also a second-hand store so there were lots of cut-price phones, tablets and other digital goodies in the window. The name of the shop was written in big black print against a friendly pink background. Underneath was a poster declaring 'cash with a smile,' next to a picture of an old-style pound note with the Queen grinning on it.

By midday Quids In was heaving with people, but when Hayley got there it was still early morning and the steel shutters were down. She pressed the intercom.

'Who is it?' Mary's voice asked on the speaker.

'It's Hayley.'

'I didn't expect you yet. Give me a minute to open up.'

Hayley waited nervously as the shutters over the entrance were raised. Mary grinned through the glass, showing off the perfect teeth that Hayley admired so much. She knew it was a bit daft to like someone's teeth, but they showed how Mary was always careful to be turned out right. She never had a hair of her dyed blonde head out of place and always wore a skirt suit. Hayley hoped to be like Mary Lewis some day.

When Hayley got inside, she saw a teenage boy sitting with his feet up on the counter, his fingers madly tapping away at a mobile phone. He was so engrossed in what he was doing that he didn't even look up.

'Don't worry about him,' Mary said with a cheery smile as she put her arm round Hayley's shoulders and led her further into the shop. 'That's my nephew, Carl. He's taking a bit of a breather from school.'

Ah, so Mary had another Jamie on her hands.

'Fancy a cuppa?' she offered. She turned and walked over to a small kettle set on a round tray with two cups, a bowl of sugar and a carton of milk.

Hayley shook her head. All of a sudden she

felt tongue-tied. How was she going to tell this good woman that she'd lost her money? A thousand pounds. The best thing to do was to just say it.

'Mary, I had a bit of a problem last night.'

The other woman didn't turn round as she asked calmly, 'What type of problem?'

'I'd collected most of the money and was on the final leg of my rounds when I got jumped and robbed.'

Mary placed a teabag in a blue mug. 'Are you all right, dear?'

Hayley breathed a heavy sigh of relief. She'd been right to believe that Mary would understand. 'He roughed me up a bit, but it was only my back that got bruised.'

Mary poured milk into her cup, but didn't add any sugar. She picked up the boiling kettle and finally turned to face Hayley. She still wore a smile but it looked like it had been set in stone. She turned towards her nephew. 'Carl, will you hold the kettle for me a minute?'

Carl placed his mobile carefully into his trouser pocket and took the kettle from his aunt. Mary's eyes never left Hayley. 'You'll just need to come in the back and sign some documents. Company policy.'

Mary led the way into the back of the shop.

They entered a corridor, which didn't fit the bright, breezy look of the storefront. It was dark and dingy with so much dust in the air that Hayley sneezed.

Mary pushed open the door to the office. But she didn't go in. Instead she said, 'After you, love.'

Hayley stepped inside. A brutal-looking thug of a man sitting in a swivel chair raised his head. She didn't like this. She turned round to find Mary and her nephew blocking her exit. Hot steam wafted from the kettle Carl held in his hand. Mary shut the door and turned the lock.

A frightened Hayley looked wide-eyed at Mary. All the kindness in the other woman was gone.

'Wh—' Hayley gulped, her eyes swinging to the kettle. 'What's going on?'

Mary broke the deathly silence, her voice strong, like she was addressing a conference. 'Hayley, I want to introduce you to my brother Bobby who owns half of the business.' Her voice turned nasty. 'She's told me some cock-and-bull story about being robbed last night. Says someone beat her up and took a grand off her—'

Mary never finished because her brother

shoved himself to his feet, making his chair fall with a crash. Hayley started quaking when she saw the size of him. He was a mountain of a man. All thick neck, thick arms and bone-crusher hands. He glared at her. 'What have you done with my money?' His voice was husky and surprisingly soft.

What was he talking about? Hayley stared back at him as if he had two heads. 'Someone attacked me and cut my money belt off with a knife. Do you want to see the bruises on my back?'

Only when Bobby growled like a dog ready to pounce did Hayley realise she should've watched her tone. But it was too late. When he stormed round the desk she knew she was in big trouble. She desperately tried to push her way past Mary and the kid with the kettle, but their bodies were a wall. She looked around desperately. No way out! No way out!

Bobby snarled as he reached her. She let out a loud scream when his arms clamped round her waist, lifting her off the floor as if she weighed nothing. She kicked him hard in the shin, but he showed no pain. When she tried to hit him again, he waved her around like a rag doll. He slammed her back down on to the desk. The bruises from last night's attack burst into pain – a whole new agony.

He pinned her arms to the desk. His face was one of the worst things she'd ever seen. It was twisted so purple with rage the blood vessels stood out everywhere.

His voice was still soft as he said one word: 'Carl.'

The teenager sauntered over. He looked down at Hayley with no pity in his eyes. He raised the kettle full of boiling water. 'Shall I do her face?' The excitement in his voice was sickening.

Bobby said, 'I'll make him do it if you don't tell me what really happened last night.'

'But I have,' Hayley called out loudly.

'What a shame,' came Mary's voice from the back of the room.

Carl moved the kettle towards her face. Tipped it forwards. Hayley squeezed her eyes tight shut. Full of dread, she waited and waited for the scalding liquid to burn her skin. But all she felt was warm water, cooled by the air, seeping on to her neck. She dared to open her eyes to find that the kid had poured water on the table near her head, leaving it to spread towards her.

'I swear, on my daughter's life, I wasn't involved in the attack.'

'Carl,' Mary ordered. The teen backed off. 'I believe her.'

Bobby shoved his face close to hers. 'Listen up and listen good. I don't care what you have to do, but you better have my money back here by four.'

'If you don't,' Mary warned, 'we're not coming after you. It will be your daughter.'

# 4

10 a.m.

Hayley finally stopped walking after five minutes and leaned heavily against a wall, her heart pumping away like crazy. She still couldn't believe what Mary, her brother and their nutcase of a nephew had done. Mary had seemed like such a nice lady. How wrong Hayley had got *that*. Now they wanted their money back by four. She checked her watch. She only had six hours to do it or else . . . She was almost sick as she pictured that kettle coming – not towards her face, but Lily's.

What was she going to do? Her brother's words spun in her head:

*'Adam. He'll know who did it. And if he can't find out who attacked you, he might give you the money.'*

Hayley shook her head. There was no way she was going to her ex-boyfriend. She'd have to get the money another way. But how? Her mind ticked over, trying to come up with an answer. A light bulb in her head lit up. She had an idea.

She checked her watch again.

10:10

She had to move fast.

Ten minutes later, Hayley rang the bell on her friend Sharon's front door. Sharon lived on the next estate, on the second floor of a small block of flats. Sharon was her best friend and always good for a laugh. They'd met at school aged eleven. They'd done everything together, including getting involved in crime. And they'd been arrested together that last time. And had been sent to different prisons. While Hayley had found out she was pregnant in prison, Sharon had left behind her two-year-old son. Nanna Lisa had taken care of Lily, but Sharon had no one to look after her boy and he'd ended up in care. Sharon had fought hard to get her son back. Just like Hayley, she'd vowed to go straight.

'Hayley,' Sharon said when she opened the door, her face breaking into a wide smile as she welcomed Hayley in. She was pretty and small with super-soft skin and jet-black curly hair.

Unlike Hayley, Sharon had managed to find a good job after getting out of prison. Her sister had fixed her up with a job at a travel agency.

So Hayley wasn't surprised to see Sharon's packed rucksack near the electric fire in the sitting room. Sharon was always flying here and there on cut-price holidays, a perk of her new job.

The sitting room was filled with things that showed how well her friend had turned her life around since leaving prison. There was a gleaming cream leather sofa with plump cushions on it, a television with a satellite box and a cabinet with shining glasses and bottles inside. And so much more. Hayley felt a stab of envy.

*I wish I could give Lily a home like this.*

As if reading Hayley's mind, Sharon put a soothing arm round her shoulders. 'You'll have a place like this one day. Just you wait and see. You've already found yourself a job—'

Hayley cried out, 'But that's the problem.' She turned and looked her friend in the eye. 'I've made a big mistake, Sharon.'

Sharon frowned in concern and led her to the long sofa to sit down. 'Tell me what's happened.'

Hayley poured out her story. 'If I don't get their money to them by four, they'll come after me and Lily.' She shivered.

Sharon took Hayley's hand and squeezed it

gently. 'This isn't your fault. All you did was try to find a decent job so you can look after Lily.'

Hayley licked her lips, upset. 'I don't think I'm going to find out who did it. I need to get my hands on some cash.' She hated doing this, but what choice did she have? 'Can you lend me a grand?'

Sharon whistled, her eyes widening. 'That's a lot of money.' For some reason her gaze darted to her rucksack. 'But maybe—'

Before she could finish, the doorbell rang. She squeezed Hayley's hand again before she stood up. 'Don't worry. We'll get this sorted out.'

As Sharon left the room, Hayley gazed after her with love brimming in her eyes. They had been through some tough and hard times and Sharon had remained a loyal friend. Hayley admired her so much for what she'd made of her life. If anyone could help her out of this mess, it was going to be Sharon.

Sharon closed the door, but she didn't come back into the sitting room. Instead Hayley heard another set of footsteps as Sharon took someone into her bedroom. Their voices came loud and clear through the thin walls.

'Are you all packed and ready to go?' It was a man's voice. Low and gruff.

'Yes. Billy will be staying with my mum as usual.'

'I don't care what you do with your son. That isn't my business.' Hayley tensed in her seat. She didn't like the sound of this man at all. Why was he being so mean?

She got up and made her way to the sitting room door, intending to offer help if her best friend needed it. But the voice started up again and stopped her in her tracks.

'All I care about is you getting that package delivered on time,' the man was saying. 'The boss says there's a nice bonus in it if you can get it done by tonight.'

Package? Hayley frowned. Why was Sharon delivering a package? Who was the boss? The only boss Sharon had was at the travel agent's.

Sharon's soft laughter came through the wall. 'Don't worry, I always get the job done on time.'

'The boss wanted to ask a favour . . .' Hayley strained to hear the rest, but couldn't because his voice was too quiet to make out the words.

Hayley was totally confused and very anxious. Her gaze fell on Sharon's rucksack. Before she knew what she was doing, she found herself walking across to it. She frowned. Maybe Sharon had to deliver a package for someone from the travel agent's while she was on holiday? But a sixth sense told her that wasn't the case.

She knew she shouldn't do it, but she was worried about Sharon. She listened carefully to make sure the hum of their voices was still coming from the other room. She glanced at the half-open door, then dropped to her knees next to the packed bag. She reached out to touch it, but her hands froze in mid-air.

*You shouldn't be doing this*, she warned herself.

*But what if Sharon's in trouble?* another voice in her head said.

Hayley listened to the second voice and her hands landed on the bag. One steadied the rucksack as the other slowly pulled back the zip. Her heart began to race and sweat glistened along her hairline. The zip squeaked. Oh no! Hayley's hand froze. She leaned towards the wall. She could still hear the voices. She touched the zip again. Very, very slowly, a little at a time, she moved it . Down, down, down it went until finally it came to the end. She was almost too scared to look.

She pulled the top open and peered inside with troubled eyes. She flinched at what she found. If Sharon was going on holiday, there would be clothes and other travel things, but there weren't. Instead there was a large blue package.

'What are you doing in my bag?'

Hayley jumped to her feet when she heard Sharon's furious voice behind her.

Sharon marched across the room, her eyes flashing. She pushed past her, leaned down and quickly closed the rucksack. The zip made a hissing, scratching sound that felt like it was going all the way down Hayley's spine.

Sharon shoved her fists on her hips. 'What gives you the right to stick your nose into my things?'

Hayley stood her ground. 'Where did you get that blue package from?'

'It's none of your business,' her friend snapped back.

'That man who was just here, I heard him talk to you about delivering a package. Is that it?' Hayley stayed calm. The last thing she wanted was to have an almighty row with her best friend.

Sharon pushed her fingers nervously through her curly hair. 'That was my boss from the travel agency—'

'I don't believe you,' Hayley snapped. 'I know when you're telling the truth and when you're not. You're not.'

Sharon's hands fell limply by her sides as if all the life had drained out of her. 'I couldn't do it, Hayley. My sister did find me a job in a travel agents.' Her mouth twisted. 'But do you know what the job was? In the kitchen making cups of tea and being a general dogsbody. It paid a pittance. I've been working for Mary Lewis and her brother.'

'Oh, Sharon.' She really felt for her friend. 'I didn't know you were collecting money for them as well.'

Sharon looked at her, astonished. 'You really must be staying away from the old life or you'd know. Everyone else around here does.'

Hayley was perplexed. 'Know what?'

'That the Lewises are the ones bringing the drugs in. I don't work for the travel agents. I work for the Lewises as a courier.'

Shock hit Hayley hard. She couldn't believe what Sharon was saying. They had vowed to go straight for the sake of their children. All this time her best friend had been lying about where she was getting her money. Suddenly the things in the room didn't look all bright and new. They looked dirty.

'But why?' Hayley asked, her voice showing her hurt.

'Because I need *real* money to put clothes on

32

my son's back. To put *real* food on the table.' Sharon's voice lowered. 'I can help you get that money you need so quickly. The guy who came round said they need another courier. You can do this job, pay the Lewises by four and then walk away. Cash in hand. So easy.'

*So easy. So easy.*

The words swirled around Hayley's brain and began to play tricks on her. It was so tempting. *All you have to do is deliver one package and then you're scot-free. The Lewises get their money back and you and darling Lily are safe. Easy.*

But it wasn't easy. If she did this, she'd never be able to look her daughter in the eye again or at herself in the mirror.

Hayley shook her head. 'I'm never going back to that life.'

She twisted round and walked briskly out of the room and towards the door. But as she turned the latch Sharon's voice made her stop.

'You do know what you've been collecting for the Lewises, don't you?'

Hayley half turned. 'Money that people have borrowed from them. Now, after the way they treated me, I know they're loan sharks.'

Now it was Sharon's turn to shake her head. 'All the money is drug debts people owe them.'

33

'No, no, no,' Hayley's mind screamed. If her probation officer found out about this she'd be back in prison, banged up away from Lily. How could she have been so stupid?

# 5

'I'd like to arrange a loan,' Hayley said to the woman behind the bank teller's window, praying that her voice didn't sound as shaky as she felt inside.

She was still stunned at finding out what the money was really for. If Mary and Bobby Lewis hadn't been pursuing her, she would've been pleased that someone had robbed her. The thought of being involved in anything to do with drugs made her sick to her stomach. And Sharon . . . She grieved to think of her friend going back to a life of crime. Sharon would get caught – you always did sooner or later – and then what would happen to her son? If he went into care again, she might not get him back a second time.

Hayley had decided that the only way out of this mess was to do it the honest way – come to her bank for a speedy loan. They had to give it to her. She didn't know what she'd do if she

35

was shown the door. She'd put on her best suit so she looked the part, not like the time she'd come here to open an account. She'd wanted to put money aside for Lily's future. She'd turned up in her tracksuit looking like a woman who'd just got out of prison, which of course she was. No wonder the woman who'd helped her open the account kept giving her funny looks. But then again, no one had the right to treat anyone like riff-raff just because of their clothes.

But Hayley hadn't made the same mistake this time. She needed that loan and if that meant dressing to impress she'd do it.

'Have you made an appointment?' the woman asked.

Hayley gave a single shake of her head, but added, 'I've got an account here, so I didn't think I needed to make one.'

'It's always best to make an appointment. You'll have to wait if you want to see someone.'

The one thing Hayley didn't have was time. But what could she do? She sat in one of the soft blue chairs and waited. And waited. Her palms started sweating. She couldn't stop glancing at the large clock on the wall.

11:05

11:09

She started rocking slightly in the chair. The wait was killing her. Her heart started beating so fast she thought it was about to jump out of her chest.

11:16

11:21

*Come on, come on, come—*

Hayley shot to her feet. This was a complete waste of time. She marched towards the door.

'Miss Evans?' someone called behind her as the automatic doors swept open.

Hayley swung round to find a good-looking man, of about her age, in a smart grey suit, searching for her. She let out a sigh of relief and hurried over to him. 'I'm Hayley Evans,' she introduced herself in a rush.

He smiled, bringing a sparkle to his attractive face. 'I'm Brian. Let's talk in here.'

'Here' was a private room tucked in a corner. A see-through wall on one side looked on to the main bank floor. Brian tucked himself behind a desk with a computer on it.

'I need to borrow some money urgently,' Hayley said as soon as her bottom touched the chair facing him.

'How much were you thinking of borrowing?'

Hayley's mouth went dry. She swallowed. 'A thousand pounds.'

He pulled open a drawer and placed some forms on the desk. 'You'll need to apply—'

Hayley interrupted in surprise. 'What? I can't just tell you and you add it to my account or something?'

His friendly manner fell away. 'I'm afraid it doesn't work like that. The bank needs to check that the money will be paid back.' He popped his smile back on. 'The forms just ask you to tell us about yourself. Things like your salary, the names of the places you've worked at for the last five years—'

'Five years?' Hayley slumped back in her chair. Of course, the bank would want to know where she'd been working. She should've guessed. 'And what if I haven't worked anywhere for the last five years?'

He touched the forms with his fingertips. 'The bank fully understands that many women will have been at home looking after their children. If that's how it is, all you have to do is say so on the form.'

As she stared at the forms, she could feel her past taking a seat in the room as well.

*Go on*, her inner voice urged, *sign the papers. He's already given you a way to get the money. Just pretend you've been a stay-at-home mum and hey presto, the money will be yours.*

Hayley reached eagerly for the forms and the pen he was offering her. She placed the tip of the pen on the paper, but her hand wouldn't move. She couldn't lie about her past. She couldn't start her new life with a tall tale. Besides, untruths had a way of coming back to bite you in very painful places.

She placed the pen firmly on the desk and looked Brian in the eye. 'The truth is, I was in prison for three years for robbery and handling stolen goods. I got out nine months ago and opened an account here. Is that going to be a problem?'

The smile on Brian's face turned to an expression of horror. He looked at her as if she'd turned up to rob the bank. Well, that was how it seemed to Hayley. It made her angry. Very angry indeed. What a fool she'd been to come here in the first place.

She stood up so fast she nearly knocked her chair over. 'I'm tired of lying to try and get a break.' Each word cracked with the fury of a whiplash. 'When I got out of prison it didn't take me long to realise that there aren't many people willing to give an ex-con a second chance.'

Brian opened his mouth to speak but Hayley charged on. 'Do you know what happens to people when they get out of prison? No one will give you a decent job. No one will give you a roof over your head.' She let out a mocking laugh. 'And no one will give you a loan. How the hell are people like me going to make a fresh start if people like you won't give us a chance?' Her voice choked in her throat. 'I wouldn't be here now begging for help if someone had just given me a chance. Given me an honest job. I need that loan . . .'

On the verge of tears she turned sharply, flung the door wide and stalked away.

'Miss Evans, I can assure you . . .' Brian called after her.

Yeah, and he could assure off, and piss off, as far as she was concerned. Hayley didn't turn back. She only stopped when the air outside dropped a layer of cold over her skin. The dark clouds above looked like rain. She took in a deep shot of air to steady her nerves. Focus, focus, focus, she told herself. She checked her watch.

11:40

She needed an answer. Now.

*Adam. He'll know who did it. And if he can't find out who attacked you he might give you the money.*

Her brother's words still haunted her. Maybe

she should go to her ex-boyfriend? No. She shook her head. Hayley would rather cut out her tongue than speak to Lily's father.

She'd met Adam five years ago when she was out raving with her mates in a nightclub in east London. She'd seen him around the estate but had never talked to him before. She should've known he was trouble straight away. What man in his right mind came up to a girl and started dancing with her as bold as brass without asking her first? Of course she wasn't interested, but he hadn't taken any notice. She'd tried her best to ignore him . . . but that charming smile of his and those cheek-popping dimples made her feel light-headed and happy.

In the end, what had really won her over was the way Adam made her feel like the most special person in the world. She hadn't felt like that since her mum was alive. He'd called her 'his angel' and driven her home in his flashy car. He hadn't tried any funny stuff: no wandering hands like most men. Instead he'd walked her respectfully to Nanna Lisa's door and given her his phone number. Now that's what you called a proper gent.

It had been such bliss in the beginning. He couldn't do enough for her. He really had treated her like the girl of his dreams. Taken her to the movies, for a bite to eat, to swanky pubs and clubs; he made sure she got anything she wanted. But that had changed as he'd drawn Hayley into his world.

It started with something small. He'd asked her to look after a bag of watches for him. She'd been so in love with him that she'd done it. She'd hidden it in the cupboard under the kitchen sink in Nanna Lisa's house. It hadn't taken long before Hayley was stealing things for him. Hiding more stolen gear at her gran's. And then the cops came calling . . . Hayley felt such shame remembering that day. Her grandmother could have got into so much trouble for having stolen goods in her home.

That should've woken her up to the world that Adam was drawing her into, but it hadn't. In fact, what had happened next was Adam discovering her special talent. Adam had locked himself out and, because he kept the door very secure, there was no chance of kicking it in. When Hayley had asked if a window was open at the back of his flat, he'd been confused. After all, he lived on the sixth floor. She'd skipped off down the stairs, ignoring him calling after her. Ten minutes later she'd enjoyed seeing his shocked face when she opened his door and let him in.

He'd demanded to know how she'd done it. He was clearly impressed, and he wasn't easily impressed. She pointed at the drainpipe that ran up by the window and told him she'd come up that. She was slim, wiry and strong, with a head for heights, so climbing things was her party piece. For as long as she could recall she'd been climbing stuff – walls, trees. Climbing out the toilet window had helped her bunk off school.

Adam's eye had glinted. He'd put his arm round her shoulders and told her all about a job he had in mind. Within weeks she was earning money by breaking into the upper floors of buildings and letting Adam's crew in at the front.

That was how she got the nickname 'Monkey'. She'd hated it. But the more she told Adam not to call her that, the more he did.

And it was also how she ended up in prison. Adam and his boys had taken her to a discount warehouse and showed her the skylight. Her role was to get in that way and key in the code for the alarm system, which Adam had got from a dishonest security guard. Only after she'd tapped in the numbers and the alarm started wailing did she realise she'd got the numbers mixed up. She'd never forgotten the code –

19141945. When she finally gave up and fled the building, Adam and his crew were gone. But the police were already waiting for her.

Looking back, Hayley couldn't believe how silly she'd been. Letting a man control her to the point where she would've done anything for him. *Anything*. Well, Adam didn't control her any more and she wasn't going to let him trap her again by begging for his help.

Nanna Lisa always said, 'Fool me once, shame on you. Fool me twice, shame on me.'

Hayley finally reached The Devil's Estate, dread dogging her every step. Time was running out. In just under four hours those thugs were expecting their money back. If she didn't stump up the cash . . . She shuddered just thinking about it.

In a daze she walked around, shattered and tired. She had no idea how long she'd been walking when she found herself under the landing of a block of flats. Near her a courier van was parked up in the courtyard with its hazard lights on. And that was when she was tempted a second time.

# 6

Above her, on the landings of the flats, she heard the out-of-breath van driver panting as he called out to an old lady. 'Excuse me, dear, is number forty down here?'

'I'm afraid not. Forty's right up the top of the stairwell.'

Hayley looked up to see the driver carrying a heavy parcel. He was rolling his eyes in despair at the thought of having to walk up another three flights of stairs.

'You and me both,' Hayley thought. Despair had been shadowing her the whole day.

She walked past the van and noticed something. The back door was a few inches open. She looked upwards again. Through the frosted windows of the stairwell, she could see the smudge of the driver's red hi-viz jacket as he struggled upwards.

Hayley peeped through the gap in the van doors. Inside she saw riches that took her back

45

to the days she'd gone out stealing for Adam. There were piles of yellow courier bags both large and small. Adam had taught her that anything sent special delivery must be pricey or it would have gone in the normal post. No doubt there would be plenty of digital things – there always were. Cameras, mobile phones, laptops and computer games.

She glanced up again and saw the driver had reached the top floor.

*So easy.*

Sharon's tempting words came back to her. So easy to grab a handful of these parcels and run for it. Even if the driver saw her, he was miles away and there was no way he would catch her. No one on the estate would grass her up. Truth be told, if they'd been there, they'd do the same. And would the cops care? No way.

Hayley tried to justify what she was thinking of doing. Being honest and straight hasn't helped you at all. Look how the man in the bank treated you: like you shouldn't breathe the same air as him.

*So easy.*

Grab the bags.

Run.

Hide behind a wall.

Open up.

See what you've got.

It was a crook's Christmas day. And Hayley knew all the places where stolen goods were taken off your hands, no questions asked. The endless cycle of nicking, dealing, receiving and fencing.

*So easy.*

For a few moments, Hayley went on looking through the gap in the van's doors; she might not get enough money to cover what had been stolen but it was a start. The world helps those who help themselves. Here was a real chance to help herself.

She looked up again. The driver was knocking on number forty.

Hayley threw open the door. She felt like a dieter faced with cheap doughnuts. She grabbed the side of the van. Go on. She hitched her leg inside.

GO ON!

But she couldn't. Wouldn't. It didn't matter what fix she found herself in, this stuff didn't belong to her. It was stealing, plain and simple. Was this how she was going to bring Lily up? Teach her to rip off people if she was in a tight spot? One false move, that was all it would take to send her back to prison.

Hayley pulled her leg back and dropped her hands. Then she slammed the doors shut.

She moved away and yelled up to the driver, 'Always lock your doors when you're on this estate. I've closed them for you.'

He gave her a grateful smile. 'Thanks, love.'

Hayley thought she'd feel relief. Instead she felt like crying.

'Hayley, honey,' Nanna Lisa called from the doorway of the community centre five minutes later.

'Oh no,' Hayley mumbled under her breath.

Her grandmother was the last person she wanted to see. She'd want to know why Hayley was wearing her best suit. But seeing how sad she looked, Hayley couldn't just walk away from her. Poor Nanna Lisa. It was such an upsetting day for her. The community centre's funding had been cut, so it was cutting back on some of its activities. It had decided to close the afternoon events it put on for the older folk on the estate. This had caused an outcry, but no one had the money to keep things going. The shame of it was that they didn't really need a lot of money. Only five thousand pounds.

So Nanna Lisa and her old friends were holding a goodbye party later on when their group came together for the final time. It was good to know that so many had turned out to help. Hayley wished those people who only had bad words to say about the estate could see it now. Sure, it had its share of people you wouldn't want to meet down a dark alley at night, but most people who lived here had hearts of gold. It wasn't right that it was known as The Devil's Estate.

'Where are you going dressed like that?' Nanna Lisa looked Hayley up and down. 'Off to see the Queen?'

Although Nanna Lisa was trying to joke, Hayley could see tears in her eyes. 'Nan, you OK?'

Nanna Lisa's lips trembled as she tried to sniff the tears back. 'I still can't believe the council won't cough up the cash for our group. Many of my friends will be stuck indoors now. We have socials here, bingo. We make sure everyone gets a hot meal when they're too frail to cook for themselves.' A lone tear tumbled down her cheek. 'Rachel keeps saying her great-nephew who works at the bank will help, but it hasn't happened. Watching this place close is like watching my dreams turn to dust.'

Hayley hugged her grandmother tight; she knew it was hard for her to talk about what was happening. Finally Nanna Lisa pulled back, wiped her eyes and gave a shaky smile. 'Mind you, I recall that time Mr Johnson and Mr Ali started fighting over Mildred. She was seventy-one and they were both eighty. You should've seen them going at it with their Zimmer frames.'

They both chuckled. 'You'll be there later, won't you, love?' her gran asked.

'I wouldn't miss it for the world,' Hayley said. *That's if the Lewises don't catch up with me because I don't have their money.*

Nanna Lisa's face turned serious. She leaned in and whispered, 'What's happening with that money business?'

Hayley plastered on a false smile and patted her nan's hand. 'All sorted out,' she lied. She didn't want Nanna Lisa worrying over her when she was so upset about the community centre. 'Mary Lewis was so understanding.' The words almost choked her.

A broad smile brightened Nanna Lisa's face. 'I was so worried about you and Lily.'

'Where is Lily?' Hayley asked. Her grandmother collected Lily from half-day nursery and often took her to the community centre afterwards.

'She's with this lovely lady who came down to help us set up for the party. It gladdens my

50

heart to see how much support we have. I'll go get Lily.'

Hayley tried to stop her because the clock was tick-tocking away to four o'clock – but Nanna Lisa was already gone. She came out of the centre followed by the 'lovely woman', who was holding Lily in her arms. It was Mary Lewis.

Hayley was so stunned she couldn't move for a moment.

Mary Lewis spoke. 'What a gorgeous girl you've got.' Her voice appeared all light and fluffy but it couldn't hide the menace. Innocent Lily lay with her head in the crook of Mary's neck, smiling shyly up at her mum's abuser. 'Now, if I had my own little Lily, I'd make sure I did everything in my power to keep her safe.' Mary tapped her finger gently on Lily's nose, making her squeal with delight.

Hayley's face darkened with rage and she held her arms out to her daughter. 'Baby, come to Mummy.'

Lily set her face in the stubborn look she wore when she didn't want to do something. But when she caught the stern expression on her mum's face, she wriggled down and came to her. Hayley clutched her tight.

'You stay away from my family,' Hayley spat.

'Hayley!' Nanna Lisa scolded, not understanding what was happening.

The other two women ignored her. Mary stepped closer to Hayley. Her face was as hard as steel. 'Four this afternoon or it won't be me seeing more of your family. It'll be Bobby. With a baseball bat.' With the nasty threat hanging in the air she waltzed off.

Alarmed, Nanna Lisa asked, 'Hayley, what the hell's going on?'

Smoothing her hand over Lily's hair, as if making sure her daughter was really there, she answered, 'That's Mary Lewis. I haven't got it sorted out, Nan. She and her brother threatened me. They want their money back by four. They're the ones flooding the estate with drugs, too.'

Nanna Lisa covered her mouth in distress. Hayley carried on. 'I didn't want to worry you earlier.'

'Oh, Hayley,' Nanna Lisa gasped, 'what's the world coming to? What can I do to help?'

Hayley lowered Lily to her feet. Nanna Lisa took her great-granddaughter's hand protectively in her own.

Hayley said, 'I need to get this sorted out once and for all.'

Her grandmother frowned. 'Don't do anything silly, love.'

'I won't.'

But Hayley knew she was about to do the most foolish thing of all.

# 7

1 p.m.

Hayley felt nervous as she looked up at The Devil's Playground. That was what most people called the sixth landing of Bridge House. It seemed like any other block from the outside. Squat and long, built of brown bricks, with white balconies that had long since turned grey. Most of its flats housed families trying to live a good life, but the top floor was different. The sixth floor was scary and dangerous. Many of the flats had been turned into drug dens and brothels. Young men roamed the landings, ready to use fists and knives to protect their patch. Even now Hayley could feel hidden faces watching her. A shiver crawled down her spine. It was whispered that even the police were reluctant to come here. But Hayley didn't have a choice.

'I can do this,' Hayley whispered, trying to give herself courage.

She lowered her eyes and walked forward to

the steel lift. She pressed the button. The doors opened with a loud thumping sound. Hayley waited for a second and then stepped inside. The back was spray-painted in colourful graffiti. It would have looked stunning in an art gallery, but here it was creepy.

When she reached for the button to the sixth floor there wasn't one. Instead there was a round, black hole like a bullet wound. Hayley was annoyed with herself. She should have remembered how you got to the sixth floor. She had once been in and out like it was her second home. The Devil's Playground was run like its own country, with its own rules, cut off from the rest of the estate.

Hayley took the lift to the fifth floor and got out. The way to the sixth floor was barred by a large mesh gate that resembled a cage. On the wall was a black keypad. Only those in the know had the code. Hayley tapped it in. The door made a hissing sound and clicked open. Hayley pulled it back, then froze.

'Don't do this,' the voice inside her screamed. 'This is a bad place. You of all people know that. Get out of here now.'

Taking that first step would mean going back into a wicked world she had vowed to leave behind. But if she didn't do it those evil loan sharks would come looking for her. And for Lily . . .

Hayley took the first step. And the second. And the next. She kept going until she saw two lookouts watching her with hard, cold faces from the top of the stairs. They were young, no older than sixteen, but held their bodies in a cocky way that showed they'd been in the crime game a long time. They were wearing the same type of dark hoodie as her attacker had. One of them wore designer tracksuit bottoms and trainers. His hood was up, and there was a silver ring piercing his bottom lip. He puffed away on a joint, filling the stairwell with clouds of weed perfume. The other wore black jeans and his hair was in a messy style that made Hayley think of a caveman.

'What do you want?' asked the one with the hoodie over his face.

But it wasn't a he. It was a she. This didn't surprise Hayley. There were plenty of girls as well as boys who were on a one-way track to trouble.

'Yeah, what do you want, Granny?' the other sniggered.

Hayley supposed she did look old to them. They probably thought they'd be teenagers for ever. Hayley should know – she had thought that too at one time. Thought that she would stay young always, without a care in the world as she slipped deeper and deeper into the darkness of crime. Her wake-up call had been giving birth to her darling Lily. Hayley prayed that these two teenage thugs would get their own wake-up call and change their lives for the better.

'I've got a delivery,' Hayley lied. She didn't have any choice but to spin a story to get on to the sixth floor.

'Oh, yeah?' The girl came down the steps and stopped very close to Hayley. She pulled hard on her spliff and blew the smoke into Hayley's face.

Hayley didn't move. She wanted to. Wanted to grab this girl by the scruff of the neck and show her all about being tough. That's what the old Hayley would have done. She'd been known for using her fists to deal with problems. Just thinking about all the people she'd thumped over the years filled her with shame. She wasn't going to go back to that. Well, not unless this girl made her. She had to get on the sixth floor.

Hayley set her face to show no fear. 'That's right. And the person waiting for me won't take too kindly to me being held up.'

The girl curled her lip, the ring in it shining. 'So who are you delivering to?'

Hayley stood her ground. 'You know the rules. You don't ever snitch about anybody else's business.' She arched an eyebrow. 'How's it going to sound to my contact if I tell him you wanted me to grass? The word's going to get around that you don't know when to keep this,' Hayley tapped her nose, 'out of other people's business.'

The girl's face paled. She didn't look so cocky any more. No one who worked the sixth floor wanted to be known for sticking their nose in where it wasn't wanted.

'What's going on?' a rough male voice asked from the top of the stairs.

Hayley looked up to see a man in his twenties wearing sunglasses. He had a cigarette in one hand and the lead of a pitbull in the other. The dog's beady dark eyes fixed on Hayley and it started to snarl, straining against its lead.

'She says she's got a delivery,' the girl said, blinking nervously.

The dog whimpered as the man pulled tight on its lead. He nodded at the girl. 'Well, let her come up, you dope,' he told her.

The girl quickly shifted to the side so Hayley could go on up the stairs.

'Thanks,' Hayley said.

But, as she took a step down the landing, the man grabbed her arm and twisted her back towards him. Up close, he smelt of stale beer.

'Not so fast,' he snarled. 'Rules have changed. You need to show me your package before you go any further.'

Hayley swallowed. She felt trapped. She should have realised that security would be much tighter after the police raid last month. She hadn't made a fake package; she hadn't thought she'd need to.

Hayley knew that the game was up. 'I don't want any trouble,' she said, grit in her voice.

'Trouble?' he said, copying her voice. He turned to his friends with a cocky laugh. 'Oh, I've got trouble for you, darling, right here in my pants.' He cupped his hand over his crotch, then leaned in and sniffed her. There was a dreamy look on his face like she was the latest drug on offer.

All those years of learning how to defend herself rushed through Hayley's mind. She raised her hand and slapped him hard across the face. The teenage lookouts gasped and the dog started jumping and yapping, spit frothing from its mouth.

'You stupid little . . .' The man slammed her into the brick wall.

Hayley felt stunned. The air whooshed out of her body. He raised his fist. Hayley squeezed her eyes closed and waited for the blow to fall. Waited for the bone-crushing pain to burst through.

But it never came. A voice down the landing yelled, 'You put one finger on her and you're a dead man!'

Hayley quickly opened her eyes. Her attacker jumped back like he'd been burned. He was staring at a tall man in the doorway of a nearby flat. His face drained of blood as he stuttered, 'I'm sorry . . . I didn't—'

The man didn't let him finish. 'Get out of here.'

He didn't need telling twice and left at speed.

Hayley took in a deep breath, drawing in the courage to help her do what she had to do next. She pulled herself away from the wall, breathing more easily. Then she carried on walking down the landing until she reached the man in the doorway. The man who ran The Devil's Playground. He leaned against the door frame, looking like he didn't have a care in the world.

There was a moment of silence as they gazed at each other. Finally he said, 'I wasn't expecting to see you around here any more, Monkey.'

Hayley's face heated up with shame at having to do this. 'Hello, Adam. I need your help.'

# 8

The last place on earth Hayley wanted to be was inside Adam's flat. But time wasn't on her side and she needed someone who knew the estate like they knew the back of their own hand. And Adam knew it like he'd built it himself.

'You'd better come in, then.' Adam moved to one side, inviting her in.

Hayley held back for a few seconds. Stepping over the doorstep would take her back to a world she'd sworn on her daughter's life to leave behind forever. Fear gripped her so hard that she almost turned and ran. This was her worst nightmare. But she didn't have a choice. Her choices had run out when Mary Lewis had held her precious daughter in her arms.

Hayley went into the flat. She stopped when she reached the sitting room. The room was filled with things that proved Adam liked the good things in life. There was a huge widescreen TV mounted on the wall, and a corner table nearby with a laptop hooked up to mini speakers. The leather three-piece suite looked new. The carpet was deep and cream. In the centre of the room was a black fluffy rug.

Hayley couldn't help the twist of her mouth. While she was in prison, her belly growing big with his child, Adam had been living the high life. 'I see you've been taking care of yourself.'

Adam lifted an eyebrow. 'If you've come round to bad-mouth me, you know where the door is.'

Hayley quickly pushed her bitter thoughts away. He was right. She wanted his help, and it wasn't going to happen if they got off on the wrong foot. They sat down facing each other.

'So how's my little girl?' Adam asked.

Hayley scoffed, forgetting her promise not to get into a row. 'You wouldn't have to ask if you'd bothered to come to see us in prison when she was a baby.'

Adam made a face, pushing out his lips. 'You know how it was. I had business to take care of. And then, when I did want to see her, you wouldn't let me.'

'Lily needs a stable life, and that doesn't include a dad who walks into it only when it pleases him.'

He looked her straight in the eye. 'I could take you to court to get access.'

Hayley snarled, 'Oh, yeah. The only time you'll be in court is when you're up in front of the judge for something.'

There was a tense silence before Adam shoved his hand in his pocket and pulled out three twenty-pound notes. He held them out to her. 'I do want to be a proper dad. Take this for the little one. Buy her something nice.'

Hayley stared at the money. She was so tempted to take it. Making ends meet was really hard. She hated asking to borrow a little from her grandmother's pension when she found her purse empty, but she couldn't see her child go without. She should take the money because he owed it to Lilly. But she wasn't going to. If he thought that waving money around every now and again made him a father, then he needed to go back to daddy school.

Hayley placed her hands in her lap. 'That's not what I came here for.' She took a steady breath. 'I've got myself into a bit of a hole and I'm hoping that you can help me out.'

Adam leaned back. 'I'm listening.'

'I've been collecting money on the never-never for some people on the estate. Anyway,

I got jumped and robbed yesterday in one of the blocks—'

Adam leaned forward, his face showing worry and concern. 'Are you OK?'

Hayley waved his question away. 'Whoever did it must've followed me and known what I was doing, because the only thing the bastard took was the money.' Hayley shivered. Just talking about it made her feel cold inside. 'I know it's a hazard of the job so I wasn't too worried about it. I thought my boss would understand.' She shook her head. 'I got that wrong. It turns out the company I'm working for is rotten to the core. Dealing drugs on the estate. I've got . . .' Hayley checked her watch, 'three hours and a bit to get their money to them.'

Adam swore savagely. 'Tell me you weren't working for those nutters Mary and Bobby Lewis.' The expression on his face said loud and clear that he knew the answer to his own question.

'I didn't know who they were,' Hayley said. 'I've been keeping my head down and walking a straight line. I couldn't get a job, so I took the first decent one someone offered me. I didn't know it involved anything illegal.'

'Why didn't you come to me sooner?' Adam asked in a softer tone.

'You know why!' Hayley waved her hands in the air to stress her next words. 'I don't want to have anything to do with you.'

That made Adam angry. 'So what are you saying? That the only time I'm worth looking up is when you want something?'

Now it was Hayley's turn to get angry. 'Do you really think I'd be here now if I could sort this out on my own?' She could feel the tears lying heavy in her eyes. But she wouldn't allow herself to cry. She looked Adam in the eye. 'All I'm thinking about is my daughter. *Our* daughter.'

She placed her hand over her heart. 'I'm trying my best to keep Lily safe. I swear, but Mary Lewis already found her at the community centre. If you're saying you don't want to help me and Lily out . . .' She got to her feet and swayed slightly with tiredness.

Adam jumped up quickly to steady her. 'Of course I'll help you. I love you, Hayley.'

For an instant, his words made her think of the good times they'd shared in the past. Walking hand-in-hand together. Watching the telly, her head lying on his shoulder, his arm tenderly round her like they were soulmates. Laughing with pure joy as he tickled her silly. But there had been so many more bad times.

He never showed his face after she'd given birth to Lily in prison. She remembered lying down in her cell while a friend whispered to her that Adam was seeing other women. Adam's love was hollow and empty. Hayley wasn't falling for that trick again. But she kept quiet. She urgently needed his help.

She broke free from his arms. 'How can you help me?'

'If something bad's happened on the estate, someone on this landing will know about it. Go home and I'll ask around.'

Hayley shook her head quickly. 'No. I'm coming with you.'

He sighed, but he could see in the stubborn set of her face that she was going to have her way.

The first three flats they visited were littered with the trappings of drug abuse . It was hard for Hayley to look in the lifeless eyes of addicts, knowing now that she had innocently helped the Lewises supply the gear that made their lives so hopeless. The dealers didn't have any news about the attack on Hayley. At the next flat, a brothel, no one knew anything either. Or the flat after that. Hayley tensed more and more with each flat they visited as she was faced with a life she'd once been part of. How could she have ever thought this was fun? A good way to live?

She felt shattered after they left the final flat. No one had any idea who had robbed her. Tiny flecks of rain drifted in the air.

'I'm sorry, babe,' Adam told her. And he did look sorry, his eyes showing a helpless misery because he wasn't able to sort it out.

Whatever she might think of him, he'd gone out of his way to help her. She linked her fingers with his to show her thanks. 'It's not your fault that I got into such an almighty mess.'

He pulled away from her grip and gently laid both hands on her shoulders. 'Maybe it is. If I'd been with you and Lily, maybe you wouldn't have needed to take a job with the kind of people who only want to use you.'

Without thinking, Hayley stepped closer to him. Her voice was smooth. 'All I've ever wanted was for you to be a father to our daughter.'

His answer was filled with regret. 'I know. And I swear to you, on my life, that's what I'm going to do.'

He pulled her close. A washed-out Hayley sighed heavily as she laid her head against his chest. For the first time that day she felt safe. So very safe.

'I'll take care of the loan sharks.' His voice felt

like a caress in her ear. 'Then I'm taking me, you and Lily on a trip to the seaside tomorrow.' Utter bliss! Hayley grinned like crazy. 'Then you can both move in with me and be a real family.' Yes! Yes! Yes! 'And we'll work together again as well as being parents to our little girl.'

Hayley's happiness skidded to a screeching halt. She wrenched away from his body as if being near him was going to burn her. 'What did you just say?'

Adam gazed at her, confused, like he didn't get what the problem was. 'I said we're going to be a family again.'

'No, the other part,' she almost shouted, some of her tough street-girl vibe coming back. 'I dare you to say it to my face.'

Adam smiled. 'Come on, baby, we made a great team. You're one of the best thieves I know. I've never seen anyone do the Spider-Man routine up a building like you. With the money we'll be raking in, we can give Lily everything she needs.'

His words were like a blow, rocking Hayley's world. That's all she would ever be to this man – a thief. A human monkey. What a bastard! And what an idiot she'd been to nearly fall for his Whitney Houston 'I will always love you' line.

She stabbed her finger at him. 'I don't need your help. *We* don't need your help. You can piss off.'

Fury was coming off her like steam as she turned away.

Adam growled after her, 'If you don't come back to work for me, I'm not going to protect you from those mad and bad Lewises.'

Hayley didn't miss a beat as she walked off.

'So be it. I'd rather meet crazy Mary with a baseball bat down a dark alley than get on my knees and beg for help from you again,' she fumed to herself.

Hayley stumbled to a stop when she saw Nanna Lisa's flat. There was a police car parked outside.

## 9

2 p.m.

They were there for her, Hayley decided as she went towards her home. Who else would the police be looking for? Maybe they had found out about her collecting drug debts. Maybe someone had seen her near the courier van. Maybe it was a past crime that had come back to haunt her. Why had she made such a royal muck-up of her life?

Hayley took a deep breath and opened the door. The first person she saw was Nanna Lisa in the hallway, her face stressed and troubled. Lily was staying at her best friend's house until Nanna Lisa collected her later for the goodbye party at the community centre.

'I'm really sorry, Nan,' Hayley said from the bottom of her heart.

'What?' Nanna Lisa looked puzzled. 'I don't know what you've got to be sorry about. The law are here—'

An officer appeared from the sitting room

and Hayley's heart sank. She had a bad history with Detective Laura Moore. Five years ago the policewoman had come knocking on Nanna Lisa's door after Adam had given Hayley the stolen watches to hide. Hayley had stashed them in the cupboard under the kitchen sink. She'd been so shocked when the detective had turned up. Somehow she'd thought helping Adam was some kind of lark. The idea that the cops would come after her had never entered her head. Detective Moore and another officer had turned the house upside down, including the cupboard under the sink. Hayley could still see Moore opening the cupboard door as if in slow motion. She'd assumed that would be the end.

But the bag wasn't there. After the police had gone, Nanna Lisa sat her granddaughter down and gave her the talking-to of a lifetime. She had come across Hayley's loot while looking for the plunger to unblock the sink. Nanna Lisa wasn't stupid; she knew exactly what those watches were. She'd taken the bag and dumped it in the canal. With disgust, she had warned Hayley never, ever to bring anything like that home again. Hayley had nodded, ashamed to think that her grandmother might've got into trouble as well. Nanna Lisa had also warned her to stay away from Adam. That she wouldn't agree to.

Detective Moore came into the hall and looked at Hayley. 'I heard you got out of prison. Still keeping your fingernails clean?'

Hayley frowned. Why would the cop be asking her if she was going straight? Wasn't she here for her? Hayley realised that something else was going on here.

Nanna Lisa gave the answer. 'The law have arrested Jamie.'

'Why?' Hayley demanded.

Detective Moore said, 'Possession with intent. We caught him and his mates on a stop and search.'

'What and how much?'

Moore stepped closer to Hayley. 'Some weed. It wasn't a lot and I would've let it go except Jamie was being very rude.'

Oh Jamie! Hayley moaned to herself. When will you ever learn to just shut up? Abusing the police was never a good idea.

Noises came from down the hallway and Hayley realised that Detective Moore wasn't alone. There were other police here, searching Jamie's bedroom. Hayley closed her eyes and stood like a statue for a moment before going to her brother's room. There were two policemen inside. The room was a total wreck. Drawers and clothes were tipped on the carpet. The sheets and duvet were in a tangle at the foot of the bed. The wardrobe had been pulled away from the wall.

'Have you found anything?' Officer Moore asked, as she followed Hayley into the room. The other two shook their heads.

'Oh, come on,' Hayley said, 'there's obviously nothing here. He's just a kid. Give him a slap on the wrist and send him home.'

Moore frowned. 'Jamie is still down the station because he's claiming we planted the drugs on him and he's totally clean. He said we could search his room, if we didn't believe him. So here we are.'

Hayley was going to murder her baby brother when she got her hands on him. 'He says more than he means sometimes,' she said. 'You know what some of these young kids are like. He's a good boy really.'

Moore didn't answer for a moment. Then she said, 'If you want him to remain a good boy, I suggest you get him to choose his friends more carefully.' She nodded to the other cops. 'That's it for today, boys.' She looked back at Hayley. 'I'll let him go and send him home.'

What a terrible day this was turning into.

After the police were gone, Nanna Lisa appeared in the doorway. Her face was pinched and worn. 'Where did I go wrong?' Her voice was hardly above a whisper as she threw her hands in the air. 'I've tried my best with both of you.' She stared at her granddaughter sadly. 'Maybe I should've let someone else bring you up.'

'Don't you ever say that!' Hayley said fiercely. Then her tone softened. 'God knows what would've happened if you'd not taken us in. You're a part of us, just like we're a part of you. I know it hasn't been easy. When I was in prison, one of the things that kept me going was knowing you'd be here for me when I got out. And your bread pudding.'

Nanna Lisa giggled and smacked Hayley on the arm, obviously pleased by the praise. Then her face turned serious again as she looked at the room. 'Let's get this cleaned up.'

'Nan, put your feet up. Get a bit of rest before your party. I'll get everything sorted in here.'

Hayley looked around at the mess, but really she was thinking about the mess her brother was making of his life. And who had taught him how to do that? She had. She'd shown him how the crime life worked. The way you thought you were getting away with it before your luck ran out. The sessions down the cop shop with the boys in blue telling you they could see you were a good girl really and why don't you 'fess up and help yourself out? The searches, the charges, the court appearances. The lawyers saying this is your last chance: next time, it's jail. The judges telling you that you've had your last chance: this time it's jail. In prison, out again, in again, out again. And now her brother was doing the same thing. It was like a never-ending cycle on a washing machine.

Hayley sighed as she began to put the room right. She started with the drawers and clothes. Only when she picked up the red Arsenal alarm clock did she see the time.

2:20

One hour and forty minutes. The noose Mary and Bobby Lewis had put round her neck was tightening. Hayley put the clock down and sank heavily on to the bed. She placed her head in her hands. What the hell was she going to do? The bank wouldn't lend her the money. She wasn't willing to steal. No way was she letting Adam sink his fangs back into her in exchange for him giving her the money.

She'd run out of options. The one thing she could do was to move Lily out of danger. Maybe she could persuade Nanna Lisa to take her to

Sheffield to see her sister, Auntie Jean. But what about the farewell party at the community centre? It wouldn't be fair to ask her gran to miss it. Nanna Lisa had poured her heart and soul into that old folks' group.

Her head was in such a muddle. What could she do? No answers came to her, so instead she just started to remake the bed. The sheet fluttered in the air as she spread it. She lifted the mattress at one end to tuck the sheet in. Lifted the mattress at the other end . . . and froze.

'No, no, no.' She wanted to deny what she was seeing, but she couldn't.

Hayley reached across and picked up the money belt. Her money belt. She knew it was hers. It was the same colour and the strap had been sliced in half.

Had her own brother attacked her?

# 10

3 p.m.

3 p.m.

Hayley couldn't let go of the money belt. She'd been holding it tightly for the last forty minutes. There were moments today when she'd thought she'd gone into shock. When a kettle full of boiling water was held ready to be tipped on her face. When a thug pressed her into the wall with his bad-tempered dog snapping and snarling at his side. But none of that could've been shock. It must've been another emotion. What she felt now was what shock really felt like.

Her blood ran hot and then cold, hot again, cold. Her mouth was so dry that her tongue felt slightly swollen. Her body was numb. And she still couldn't believe that her brother, her Jamie, would do this to her. There must be a reason for him to have the money belt. That he'd found it on his travels, dumped in a bin somewhere by the robber, and had brought it home for her. Hayley knew that was nonsense, but God, it was better than what might be the truth.

She didn't move when she heard the front door open and bang closed. Her brother was back. Jamie went straight to his bedroom. Hayley got off the sofa. She didn't knock when she reached his door, but went inside feeling only sadness and sorrow. He was lying on his bed, gazing at the ceiling. He didn't look at Hayley.

He had plenty to say, though, his voice full of bad-boy attitude. 'Yeah, yeah, yeah, so I got pulled in by the cops for a little bit of stuff – big deal.' When she didn't answer, he finally looked at her as he repeated, 'Big deal.' But when he saw her face, his features froze with worry. 'What's up?' The sound of his breath catching in his throat filled the room as he quickly added, 'Has something happened to Lily?'

Hayley wanted to yell, scream and shout at him, but she made herself calmly walk in silence across the room. She sat on his bed. Her hand seemed to be frozen around the belt. Finally she showed it to him and asked in a faint voice, 'What's this?'

He looked at it, his eyes widening in surprise. Then Jamie slumped back down on the bed and turned his face to the ceiling. 'Don't know.'

Hayley wanted to grab him and force him to face her, but instead fury filled her voice. 'It's the money belt that was stolen off me last night. That's what it is.'

He swiftly turned back to her. He wore that snarl she had come to hate so much. 'You've got no right to go snooping around my room. It's private. Go away.'

Hayley looked him in the eye, hoping he would at least be honest, but he shied away from her stare. 'I found it after the police came and turned your room over. It was under the mattress. How did it get here, Jamie?'

Again he was stuck, not knowing what to say. 'The cops probably put it there. Yeah, I reckon that's how it got there. The cops did it. They're always stitching people up.'

He looked hopeful, but she didn't miss how fear played in his eyes just like it used to when he was a kid and had done something wrong.

She let go of her emotions and yelled, '*You* stole my money? *You* attacked me?'

Jamie jumped off the bed. 'What are you going on about? I never laid a finger on you.' He stuttered, 'I'd never do that—'

'Then how the hell did you f—' She just about stopped herself from swearing. She never used bad language with her brother because she'd

79

tried hard, along with Nanna Lisa, to bring him up right. Hayley got up and waved the money belt in his face. She inhaled a huge breath. 'Just tell me how you got it.'

'All right,' he shot back, but his gaze skidded away from her. 'All right. The truth is I found it. After you told me what had happened I went out looking for it. I found it dumped in a bin near the garages—'

Hayley wasn't letting up on him. 'How did you know it was the same one?'

His face turned red. 'Are you calling me a liar?'

The resulting silence was electric. She knew what game he was playing. It was the same one he always played when Nanna Lisa or she had him in a tight corner. He used their words to twist the argument his way, making him appear the innocent and them in the wrong.

His luck had run out; she wasn't falling for it this time. 'Just tell me.'

He finally made eye contact. 'You told me the mugger cut it off you with a blade.' He pointed a finger at the money belt. 'You can see the cut marks on the belt bit.' He shook his head and defiantly folded his arms.

'So if you found it,' Hayley pressed on, 'why didn't you show it to me? Why hide it in your room?'

Jamie swallowed hard, his gaze flipping away from her. 'Well . . . well . . . I forgot to give it to you. And then I thought – what's the point? So I put it under my mattress.' His voice dropped to a whisper. 'And then I thought, I'll give it to you later.' When he finally looked at her, he pleaded, 'Why won't you believe me when I'm telling you the God's honest truth?'

He flopped back down and rolled over to face the wall. It was like talking to a child who'd stolen cake and had chocolate round his mouth.

Her voice was hard. 'You're about as good a liar as you are a thief. Jamie, I want the truth and I want it now.'

Hayley sat back on the bed, grabbed his shoulder and yanked him round. The time for her brother to stop facing up to the truth was over.

He looked sad, miserable. 'I wouldn't have done it if I'd known—'

'You pulled a knife on me, for God's sake,' she cut in. 'I was scared out of my wits. I thought I was going to bloody well die.'

His face fell. 'I was only going to use it to cut off the money belt, but then you started fighting back. I panicked.' His voice caught. 'I didn't realise you were going to be scared—'

But Hayley didn't let him finish. 'Well, here's

a reality check. That's how people feel when someone sticks a blade in their face. But I haven't got time to get into this; I need the money back. Where is it?'

For a few moments, the fact that her hands were nearly back on the money was all that mattered. Her problems were nearly over and sorting out her brother could wait. 'Where is it? I need it now.'

There was a painful silence, like the one that comes before a doctor saying, 'I'm sorry to have to tell you . . .' She said it again, more firmly this time. 'Where is it?'

'It's gone. I spent it.'

Her voice rose as she got off the bed. 'Spent it?'

'Yeah. Me and the boys are selling. I had to have some cash to buy in, didn't I? That was the stuff the cops caught me with.' Then he added, 'Don't worry, I'll get some more, sell it on and get your money back.'

Hayley had had enough. She lunged at him and grabbed him. 'You. Stupid. Stupid. Boy. Tell me who you're buying the gear off.'

Jamie shook his head. 'You know I can't do that—'

Hayley roughly dragged him close so that their faces were inches apart.

'Jamie Evans, you'd better tell me or else . . .'

'Adam just wanted a bit of help—' Her brother slammed his mouth shut tight, realising what he was saying.

'What do you mean, a bit of help?' Then she understood. 'It was him, wasn't it? Adam put you up to this.'

It all fell into place. Why Adam had been expecting her when she turned up at his flat. The way he'd offered to help her. How he'd trailed around the sixth floor asking his mates if they knew who'd jumped her. And his offer to help her out. As long she helped him out, of course. She'd been played for a fool. And he'd got her own brother to stage the robbery for him. What a piece of work!

'I can't believe this,' Hayley said quietly as she let go of her brother, who slumped back on the bed. 'You dumped me in so much crap, I can't see over the top. How could you do this to me? How many times have me and Nanna Lisa told you to stay away from him?'

'Adam was the only one there for me after you got banged up,' Jamie quickly defended himself. 'I could talk to him. He never yelled at me or told me to do this and that. All he ever did was listen. So when he needed a bit of help I gave it to him.'

'What did he tell you to do?' she asked.

Jamie swallowed hard. 'All he wants is to get you back. He said all he wanted was to be a good dad to Lily. So I watched you on your rounds for a couple of days to make sure I knew your route. Then I waited for you in Bell Tower.' His voice began to break up as he went on. 'I had to get the money off you and give it to Adam. He said you'd come to him because you'd have no one else to turn to.'

'And once I came to him, I'd see what a good guy he was,' Hayley took over. 'And then we'd ride off into the sunset hand-in-hand.' She shook her head in fury and disbelief. Why couldn't her brother see her ex-boyfriend for what he was? 'Adam's a crook, the type of crook I don't want you to become. I'm not interested in him. I've turned my back on that life. All I want is the money back.'

'What do you care?' Jamie half-sneered. 'It's not your money, is it? Let the company pay.'

She closed her eyes wearily for a few seconds. 'Yeah, I used to think that when I nicked stuff. I used to think – oh, they're insured. I used to think people should lock their homes up better if they didn't want them broken into. But you know what? I got tired of blaming other people for what I did.'

She licked her lips and carried on. 'The people I was collecting money for are a nasty lot. They want their money back and, if I don't get it for them, they're coming after your niece.'

'Lily?' His face crumbled.

'Yes, Lily.' Hayley desperately wanted to shake him again. 'A little girl who has never done a bad thing in her life. All because you can't stop thinking of yourself. You never worry about how your actions will affect the rest of us. Why can't you think of your family for a change?'

Jamie's eyes blazed at her. 'You're so wrong. All I ever think about is the family we once were. I miss her.'

'Who?' Hayley frowned, confused.

Tears filled his eyes. 'Mum. I miss her. Why did she have to die?' Huge sobs racked his body as he slumped forward.

Hayley was taken completely by surprise. All this time she'd thought that her brother was just being a nuisance and bad. That he'd been happy to bring trouble to their door, when all the time he'd been hurting. He'd been trying to deal with their mother's death the only way he knew how.

'Oh, Jamie,' she said sadly. She pulled him into her arms, feeling the shakes and tremors going through his body. She didn't speak; just let him cry his grief out.

He turned his tear-stained face to her. 'And then you left me as well.'

She frowned. 'I never left you.'

'You went to prison, Lee-Lee,' he cried, using the name he'd called her when he was a little boy. 'All the people I love always leave me behind. Dad. Mum. You.'

Hayley sucked in a huge shocked breath. She felt terrible. How had she never realised this? Instead of helping her brother deal with his grief, she'd got involved in a life of crime. He was right. How could she have forgotten about her brother when he needed her the most?

'I was wrong to leave you,' she finally said. 'It wasn't only Nan's job to look after you but mine as well.' She squeezed his arm. 'That's why I'm never going back to that life. Mum's no longer with us, but that doesn't mean we can't be a proper family again.'

Jamie looked up at her as he wiped the tears from his face. Then brother and sister sealed the promise with a smile.

The door opened, surprising them both. A furious Nanna Lisa stood in the doorway, her gaze piercing through Jamie. 'You silly, silly boy. Back in my day you'd have got a clip round the ear. But I don't believe in that kind of stuff. You've caused your big sister loads of trouble. What we need to figure out is how to get the money back from that plonker Adam.'

Hayley stood up. 'Nan, there's only one thing to do.' She checked her watch.

3:15

'And I've got forty-five minutes to do it and get the money to the Lewises.'

# 11

3:20

Hayley didn't wait for the lift but rushed up the five floors to The Devil's Playground. She punched in the access code to the sixth floor. As she headed up the stairs, she could hear shouting, yelling, laughter and the sound of a dog that didn't seem to be in a very good mood. As she reached the final step, she jumped sideways as a dog ran in front of her at full speed. She heard cheers from one end of the balcony and the dog speeding towards something at the other. Hayley stood still, unsure what was going on. A voice called the animal and it came trotting back with lumps of pink plastic between its jaws.

Hayley looked round the corner. There was a group of young lads and the girl with the pierced lip holding various breeds of dogs on leads. At the other end was a tailor's dummy propped up against a wall. It was attack practice for dogs.

88

One of the youths saw her and shouted, 'What do you want?'

'I've come to see Adam.'

She glanced at her watch.

3:22

She didn't have time to waste so she headed down the landing.

One of the youths shouted angrily behind her, 'Go on, boy! Kill her! Kill her!'

A dog howled and snarled, its paws scraping the concrete. Hayley raced down the balcony to Adam's front door and hammered on it to get in before she was bitten. But when she peeped over her shoulder the laughing boys and girl still had their dogs on leads.

Adam's door swung open. He stopped in the doorway before he spoke. 'I was hoping you'd drop by again. You look like you're about to jump out of your skin.' He looked down the landing. 'Oh, the boys are just running their dogs.'

He pulled the door back to let her in. 'I know you think I'm a first-class git, but I only want to help you and Lily.'

She walked past him and into the flat. When they got to the front room, Adam sprawled on the sofa but Hayley stood proud, her arms folded.

She spoke slowly. 'It will be four soon and I haven't got the money.'

Adam tilted his head to the side as he watched her. 'I gave you a way out, but you chose to chuck it back in my face, Monkey.'

'Don't call me—' Hayley bit out and then stopped herself. She sighed and took a step towards him. 'Look, maybe I was being a bit hasty.'

His face split into a huge smile. 'What I've always loved about you, babe – as well as your light fingers – is that you're a realist. You know when to put your hands up and say, oops I got it wrong.'

Hayley's mouth tightened. 'Is that what you want? For me to get down on my knees and beg?'

Adam chuckled. 'Plenty of time for you to get down on your knees later, you know what I mean.' He patted the seat next to him. 'Why don't you come and sit down while we work things out?'

'Adam, I don't have a lot of time. I need—'

'Sit,' he ordered.

Hayley perched on the edge of the sofa. 'All right, stop mucking about. Give me the money you said you'd loan me and I'll come and work for you again.'

Adam leaned right into her, but Hayley didn't move an inch. 'I want much more than for you to come work for me. Me, you and Lily are going to be a family.'

He kissed her long and hard. Hayley sat there and took it. She didn't respond or move away.

He wasn't best pleased when he raised his head. Then he smiled, though it didn't reach his eyes. 'Take your clothes off.'

'Are you for real?' She was outraged. 'There are people chasing me who'll take it out on your daughter if I don't turn up with a grand in . . .' she checked her watch, 'thirty-two minutes.'

'Screw the Lewises. I'll take care of them. I won't let them touch Lily.'

'Then why haven't you done it already?'

Adam curled his lip. 'Don't get in my face, Hayley. You know what they say about biting the hand that feeds—'

A fist banged loudly on the front door. 'Adders!' one of the kids yelled. 'Get out here, mate. Some man's having a go at your car.'

Adam flew off the sofa and ran to the front door, followed by Hayley. Outside, they leaned over the balcony wall. Below, a hooded youth dressed in black with a scarf over his face was smashing Adam's car with a baseball bat. The car was parked in its usual spot, in a bay meant for a senior citizen with a dodgy leg that Adam had 'borrowed' and never given back. The black car showed gashes of silver and the windows were all smashed in, glass scattered around it. Further down the landing, the boys with the dogs were looking on, unable to believe their eyes. Someone having a go at Adam's car? No one on this estate would dare even lean on it, never mind take a bat to it.

Adam looked on, shocked and furious, for a few moments before turning to the boys. 'What are you standing there for? Get after him!'

They flew down towards the stairwell. Adam was close behind them.

Hayley shouted after her ex, 'Do you want me to help?'

He stopped. 'Help? What's the matter with you? This is a man's job.'

Hayley stood on the balcony and watched as the boy with the bat ran off.

Five minutes later a fuming Adam came back. Hayley stood up.

'Did you get him?'

Adam snarled, 'My car's a total write-off. When I find that little—'

'Did you see who it was?'

He chucked his keys on the sofa in disgust.

'No. If I knew who he was, he'd be dead now.'

Hayley opened her eyes wide. 'I was so scared.'

'No need for any of that. I'm here to protect you. And our daughter.'

She shook her head. 'It's just brought back what it's really like to be around you. I'm sorry, Adam, I can't do this any more. I've got to think of Lily. Thanks for the offer, but I can't take it.'

She moved past him to get to the door, but his hand snaked out and stopped her. 'Are you going back on your promise to work for me?'

Hayley snatched her arm back. 'I'm going to go and see the Lewises and reason with them.'

Adam snorted. 'You fool. They'll eat you for dinner.'

Hayley didn't answer. She headed for the door. She didn't look back as she walked away.

Once she got downstairs she checked her watch.

3:38

Hayley started sprinting home.

'Nanna Lisa,' she called out as soon as she shut the front door.

Her grandmother was sitting bolt upright at the kitchen table. Her brother, sweating and out of breath, was on another chair in the corner, rubbing his face. He was dressed all in black. When Hayley came in, they both glanced up. She stood at the table looking solemn.

Finally her gran asked, 'So?'

A smile of pure pleasure spread across Hayley's face as she reached inside her jacket and pulled out a roll of ten-pound notes tied with an elastic band. She threw it on the table.

She looked at her brother. 'It was exactly where I remembered Adam hiding things.'

All three of them had cooked up the plan to get the money back. Hayley had at first wanted to do it on her own, using her old monkey skills to get into Adam's flat. But Nanna Lisa had, as usual, been sensible, arguing that Hayley's plan wouldn't work if he was at home. They had agreed the only way to get Adam out of his flat was to create a distraction, a trap. While Jamie attacked Adam's car, Hayley had gone into Adam's kitchen and found the money hidden behind a loose ceiling tile.

Nanna Lisa jumped up in delight and yelled, 'Whoop! High five!'

Hayley, Jamie and Nanna Lisa slapped their hands together.

Nanna Lisa turned towards the door. 'I'd better go and pick up Lily from her friend's.'

'We're not home and dry yet,' Hayley said, 'I've still got to get the money to them.'

She looked up at the clock on the kitchen wall.

Fifteen minutes left.

Hell, she'd thought she had more time. She'd only come back home to make sure Jamie was OK.

Hayley bolted out of the house, the money in her pocket.

*I'm not going to make it.* She was panicking.

# 12

3:46

3:47

3:48

Hayley ran so hard that her chest felt like it was on fire.

3:50

3:53

*I'm not going to make it. Not going to—*

Suddenly a car came out of nowhere and mounted the pavement in front of her. Oh God, the Lewises! But it wasn't them. Adam got out of the car, a different one from the precious flashy car Jamie had trashed.

'Where is it, Hayley?' he asked. His fists were balled by his side.

'I can't do this now.' She tried to dodge around him. 'Get out of my bloody way.'

But he wouldn't let her. He backed her into a corner and leaned into her, his face turning nasty. 'You think you're so clever. Distracting me by getting someone to smash my car so you can take the money.'

Hayley was about to try and get round him, but something made her stop. The time for games was over. 'I used to think I knew you so well,' she said. 'I never dreamed in a million years that you would use my own brother to try and hurt me.'

Adam shook his head. 'I wasn't trying to hurt you. I want you to come back. I want Lily back. If there's any way I can get you, Hayley, I'm going to try it.'

'Be truthful, Adam. You don't really want *me*. You want someone – anyone – who's a good thief.'

He shook his head furiously. 'You're so wrong. Don't you see, with your skills and my head we can make a life for Lily. We can buy her designer gear, toys, take her away on holiday.'

He just didn't get it. Didn't get it at all. 'When I was in prison, one of the tutors said to me I had a very special skill.' She tapped the corner of her head. 'They said I was quick-thinking. I can solve problems. I'm not a thief. Or a monkey. Maybe in the past, but not any more. Now I'm a woman who sees a rich future in front of her.

97

One day someone is going to want me to work for them because I'm smart and honest.'

Her voice cracked with emotion. 'What you did today didn't just hurt me. It hurt Lily too. One false move today and I could've ended up back in prison and lost contact with my daughter for God knows how many years. I told myself I would never beg for anything from you.' She swallowed. 'But I'm begging you to leave me and Lily alone so we have a chance at a better life.'

Adam's mouth moved, but no words came out. He shifted back from Hayley and coughed. Finally he spoke. 'I didn't realise . . .' The words got trapped in his throat.

Hayley pulled out something from her pocket and held it out to him. It was a photo of their daughter as a baby. 'I found this in your hiding place. I know that you love Lily in your way, but it can't be like this, Adam. She can't have a criminal for a father. I won't have it.'

He said nothing. He took the photo and just stared at it. Then he raised his head. 'All right, I'll go. I won't contact Jamie again either.'

He walked away, his shoulders hunched, leaving Hayley standing looking after him. She called out, 'But if you ever get out of the bad life, Lily will be waiting for you.'

She checked her watch.

4:01

She was too late.

Hayley kept running. She wasn't giving up. So what if she was ten minutes late. She had the money, which was what they really wanted. Quids In came into view. She rushed across the road. Through the window she could see Mary Lewis and her nutter nephew. Mary caught her eye and grinned.

As Hayley reached for the door the sound of sirens screeched through the air. Something told her to leave the door and keep walking. She quickly turned the next corner and watched as three police cars slammed to a halt outside the store.

The cops flooded into the shop. What the hell was going on? Her question was answered when Mary, Bobby and Carl were dragged out in handcuffs.

'You haven't got a thing on us,' Mary spat.

'There's enough evidence in that shop to put you away for a long time,' one of the cops answered.

'No one will testify against us,' Mary scoffed.

'We got a tip-off,' the officer said. 'Plus we've been watching this place for some time.'

Hayley turned away from the scene. She couldn't believe it. The Lewises wouldn't be on her back any more. Lily was safe.

She pulled out the envelope with the money. What was she going to do with a thousand pounds?

# 13

4:30 p.m.

Patsy Cline's 'Crazy' was playing when Hayley made her way from the back of the community centre into the main room. The place was done up a treat. Balloons and streamers were hanging from the wall. The bar was open and two tables were piled with food, including Nanna Lisa's yummy bread pudding. A few of the older folks were sitting down but a good many were slow dancing, some with their Zimmer frames. Hayley knew this was a sad occasion but she couldn't help smiling.

'Mummy! Mummy!' Lily shouted as she spotted her mum and flew across the room into her arms.

Hayley hung on tight. Her precious daughter was safe. If the police hadn't turned up, she didn't know what she would've done. The Lewises might still have come after Lily, if Hayley had turned up late with their dirty cash.

She put Lily down at last. 'You look like a

princess,' she said, her eyes twinkling.

An urban princess. Lily was decked out in dungarees and tiny sky-blue Doc Martens that Hayley had saved up hard to buy.

'Hayley,' Nanna Lisa shouted from where she was dancing with one of the men in the group, 'come and shake a leg.'

Hayley grinned a cheeky grin. 'When you put on some decent music.'

Nanna scoffed good-naturedly. 'You kids don't know what good music is.'

Her grandmother twisted out of her partner's arms and walked across to her. 'How did it go? Did you give them thugs their money?'

Hayley pulled her grandmother to the side so no one else could hear. 'The cops turned up and raided the place. They must've found some drugs because they cuffed the Lewises and took them away.'

Nanna Lisa gasped. 'They never.'

Hayley studied her grandmother. There was something about her face that wasn't right. 'Nan! You never called the police?'

The older woman placed her hand over her heart. 'Would I ever do anything like that?' But she winked at Hayley, giving her the real answer.

'I love you, Nan.' Hayley gave her a peck on the cheek.

Nanna Lisa waved her playfully away. 'Stop that. You're going to smudge my make-up.' Then she turned sad eyes onto the party-goers. 'I can't believe this will be the last time we'll all be together.'

Suddenly, one of the members, 68-year-old Milly Foster, rushed into the room waving an envelope. 'Look what I found in the office.'

Everyone gathered around. 'What is it?' someone asked.

Milly opened the envelope and pulled out a roll of ten-pound notes. 'It's a thousand quid.' A collective gasp went up. 'Look what it says on the front of the envelope.'

Written in black ink were the words: Well Wisher.

Nanna Lisa piped up, 'Someone has donated some money. It's not enough but maybe the council will think again about shutting the group down. I wonder who could have left it?' She looked across at Hayley, but her grand-daughter said nothing, just smiled.

'We won't need the council,' another voice insisted.

The group parted and Nanna Lisa's friend Rachel Martin made her way to the middle. But she wasn't alone. She was with . . . Hayley did a double-take. It was that handsome guy

Brian from the bank. He was holding the hand of a little boy, about the same age as Lily.

'This is my great-nephew Brian,' Rachel introduced him. 'Remember I said he was going to sort us out. He works at the bank and they sometimes give money to the community. And my Brian,' she patted him on the shoulder, beaming, 'has got the bank to stump up this year's money *and* next year's so the group can carry on.'

A huge cheer went up.

Nanna Lisa yelled at the DJ, 'Play some of that Destiny's Child. I'm in the mood to shake my booty.'

Hayley rolled her eyes. Nanna Lisa was plain crazy but she wouldn't have her any other way. As the pensioners started dancing to 'Survivor', Brian walked over to Hayley.

'How are you doing?'

Hayley's face heated up as she thought back to how they'd met. She decided to avoid the subject and asked, 'Is this your son?'

Brian nodded. 'His name's Terry. Me and his mum split up and I got custody.' He looked down at his son. 'Why don't you go with Hayley's daughter . . .' He looked up at Hayley to make sure he'd got this right. She nodded. 'Get drinks for you both, Terry.'

Terry and Lily skipped off, leaving the two adults in an awkward silence.

Brian spoke first. 'I would've given you the loan today if you'd stuck around.'

Hayley's eyebrows shot up in surprise. 'Really?'

'Yes. I was a bit of a tearaway myself in my youth. I got a lucky break when a policeman gave me a chance. I went on a training course and that's how I ended up at the bank. I worked my way up to assistant manager.'

Hayley could only gawk at him. From bad boy to assistant manager would have taken some real graft and a strong mind.

'I don't know if you'd be interested,' Brian went on, 'but I may have a job for you. My Great-Aunt Rachel told me all about you.'

'What kind of job?'

'Nothing big. We're looking for a cleaner and someone to help in the canteen. Shall we get a drink and talk about it?'

Hayley nodded and they walked over to the bar. A job in a bank? She couldn't believe it. One right move – that was all she needed to turn her and Lily's lives round.

# Thanks

I'm forever indebted to Ruth Tross, the editor of the century, Jacqui Lewis for her super editing, my fab agent Amanda Preston and the super team at Quick Reads. I would never have written this if I hadn't received Cathy Rentzenbrink's love letter – thanks Cathy! And eternal thanks to my other half, Tony, for helping with ideas and holding my hand.

# About Quick Reads

Quick Reads are brilliant short new books written by bestselling writers. They are perfect for regular readers wanting a fast and satisfying read, but they are also ideal for adults who are discovering reading for pleasure for the first time.

Since Quick Reads was founded in 2006, over 4.5 million copies of more than a hundred titles have been sold or distributed. Quick Reads are available in paperback, in ebook and from your local library.

To find out more about Quick Reads titles, visit

## www.readingagency.org.uk/quickreads

Tweet us 🐦 @Quick_Reads

**Quick Reads is part of The Reading Agency,**
a national charity that inspires more people to read more, encourages them to share their enjoyment of reading with others and celebrates the difference that reading makes to all our lives.
**www.readingagency.org.uk Tweet us @readingagency**

The Reading Agency Ltd · Registered number: 3904882 (England & Wales) Registered charity number: 1085443 (England & Wales) Registered Office: Free Word Centre, 60 Farringdon Road, London, EC1R 3GA The Reading Agency is supported using public funding by Arts Council England.

We would like to thank all our funders:

**LOTTERY FUNDED**

# Quick Reads has something for everyone

**Stories to make you laugh**

**Stories to make you feel good**

**Stories to take you to another place**

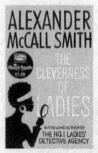

# Stories about real life

# Stories to take you to another time

# Stories to make you turn the pages

# Discover the pleasure of reading with Galaxy®

*Curled up on the sofa,*
*Sunday morning in pyjamas,*
*just before bed,*
*in the bath or*
*on the way to work?*

*Wherever, whenever,*
*you can escape*
*with a good book!*

*So go on...*
*indulge yourself with*
*a good read and the*
*smooth taste of*
*Galaxy® chocolate.*

Proudly supports **Quick Reads**

# Blood Sister
## Dreda Say Mitchell

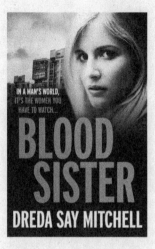

There are two ways out of Essex Lane Estate,
better known as The Devil. You make good,
or you turn bad.

Jen Miller is determined not to make the same
mistakes her mother did. She's waiting to find herself
a good job and a decent man.

Her younger sister Tiff is running errands for a
gangster and looking for any opportunity for fun
and profit. But she might just be in over her
head . . .

At least they can rely on each other.

*Can't they?*

HODDER

# Blood Mother
## Dreda Say Mitchell

1970s London has stopped swinging,
but it's not staying still.

Babs thought she had all the world ahead of her.
Then she got pregnant and the father did a runner.

Salvation comes in the form of a man who'll look
after her. Or so she thinks.

But Stan Miller is the devil in disguise . . .
and over the next twenty years, Babs will
have reason to regret she ever met him.
Can she protect her family – or will he get the
better of her?

HODDER

# Geezer Girls
## Dreda Say Mitchell

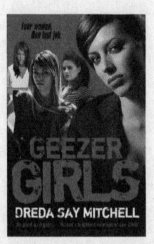

Fifteen-year-old Jade Flynn and her friends
at the Care Home were forced to work for a man
they called The Geezer. But a shocking event gives
them no choice but to run away.

10 years later, Jade is living a respectable life.
She invites her three best friends to be her maids
of honour. But someone else turns up as well –
The Geezer.

This time if they disappear they won't be
coming back . . .

**HODDER**

# Gangster Girl
## Dreda Say Mitchell

Daisy Sullivan's father was one of London's
most infamous gangsters. Haunted by his violent
death she vows to live a respectable life. That is,
until the day her mum turns up.

Daisy's mum is the head of one of London's
most feared underworld families. She draws Daisy
into their next criminal act – a bank job that turns
out to be no ordinary robbery.

Soon Daisy is running for her life and the only person
she can trust is up-and-coming gangland
bad boy, Ricky Smart.

She'll have to use every dirty trick her dad
ever taught her to stay alive . . .

HODDER

# Hit Girls
## Dreda Say Mitchell

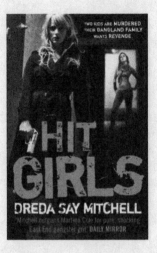

Two kids are murdered . . .

Their gangland family want revenge.

Ten-year-old twin sisters are murdered outside their school. But they aren't just anyone's kids, they're gangster Stanley Lewis' daughters.

A rival gangster is arrested, but Stanley's dad, feared villain Kenny Lewis, thinks there's more going on. So he contacts the one group of people who he trusts to help him find the truth . . .

Jackie, Anna, Roxy and Ollie. Four women with shady pasts who take the cases people don't take to the cops. They enter a world where everyone, including the Lewis family, are hiding secrets.

HODDER

# Vendetta
## Dreda Say Mitchell

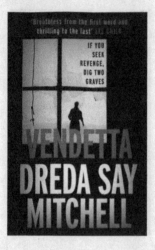

Two murders. Two different crime scenes. One killer?

Mac wakes in a smashed-up hotel room with no
recollection of what has happened. With his lover's
corpse in the bathroom and the evidence suggesting
that he killed her, Mac is on a mission to uncover
the truth and find the real killer.

But he's in a race against time with less than a day to
unravel the mystery. Still reeling from a personal
tragedy Mac isn't afraid of pain. Hot on his heels is
tenacious Detective Inspector Rio Wray. Double-crossed
and in the line of fire, Mac has to swim through a
sea of lies to get to the truth.

But only Mac knows he's been living a double life.
Can he be sure he doesn't have the blood of a dead
woman on his hands?

HODDER

# Death Trap
## Dreda Say Mitchell

Teenager Nikki Bell is the only witness to the brutal murder of two members of her family and their cleaner. She's lucky to be alive. But the murder isn't a one-off. It's part of a bigger, more violent attack planned on affluent families in the area - and now Nikki, as the only living witness, is a dangerous threat to the well-orchestrated scheme.

As the net draws tighter around the killers, DI Rio Wray must do whatever it takes to keep Nikki alive. But when you're dealing with criminals, there's no line they won't cross . . . In a kill-or-be-killed-world, who will be first to pull the trigger?

HODDER

## Start a new chapter

# The Other Side of You

## Amanda Craig

Will must run, or die. He's seen a murder,
and the gang on his estate are after him.

Hurt, hungry and afraid, he comes to an abandoned house in
a different part of the city. Behind its high fences is a place of
safety. Here, he can hide like a wounded beast. He can find
food, and healing – and learn how to do more than survive.

But when Will meets Padma, he must choose between his good
side and his bad one. For the gang he left behind is still there.
How can he live without becoming a killer?
How can he love without being a thief?

Exciting, fast-paced and different, this is a story
that keeps you reading until the last line.

Available in paperback, ebook and from your local library

Start a new chapter

# Dead Simple

## Eight killer reads from eight bestselling authors

### Edited by Harry Bingham

*Dead Simple* is a thrilling collection of short stories from some of the best crime writers around. The stories include the perfect murder and an unusual way to solve crimes. From prison cells to cosy living rooms, these dark, chilling tales will grip you with every twist and turn.

This collection includes specially written short crime fiction from Mark Billingham, Clare Mackintosh, James Oswald, Jane Casey, Angela Marsons, Harry Bingham, Antonia Hodgson and C.L. Taylor.

Start a new chapter

# A Very Distant Shore

## Jenny Colgan

**Wanted: doctor for small island. Must like boats,
the seaside and having no hope of keeping a secret ...**

Lorna lives on the tiny Scottish island of Mure,
a peaceful place where everyone helps their neighbour.
But the local GP is retiring, and nobody wants his job.
Mure is too small and too remote.

Far away, in a crowded camp, Saif is treating a little boy
with a badly-cut hand. Saif is a refugee, but he's
also a doctor: exactly what Mure needs.

Saif is welcome in Mure, but can he forget his past?
Over one summer, Saif will find a place to call home,
and Lorna's life will change forever.

Available in paperback, ebook and from your local library

# Why not start a reading group?

If you have enjoyed this book, why not share your next Quick Read with friends, colleagues, or neighbours?

The Reading Agency also runs **Reading Groups for Everyone** which helps you discover and share new books. Find a reading group near you, or register a group you already belong to and get free books and offers from publishers at **readinggroups.org**

There is a free toolkit with lots of ideas to help you run a Quick Reads reading group at **www.readingagency.org.uk/quickreads**

Share your experiences of your group on Twitter

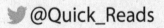 @Quick_Reads

# Continuing your reading journey

As well as Quick Reads, The Reading Agency runs lots of programmes to help keep you and your family reading.

**Reading Ahead** invites you to pick six reads and record your reading in a diary to get a certificate **readingahead.org.uk**

**World Book Night** is an annual celebration of reading and books on 23 April **worldbooknight.org**

**Chatterbooks** children's reading groups and the **Summer Reading Challenge** inspire children to read more and share the books they love **readingagency.org.uk/children**